# 강화설

UEA PUBLISHING PROJECT
NORWICH

# KANG HWAGIL

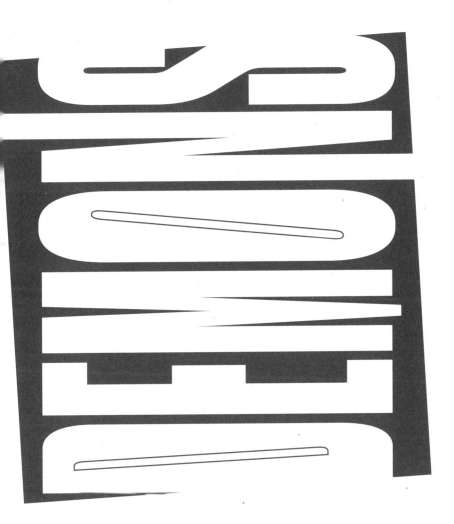

DEMONS

Demons
Kang Hwagil

*Translated from the Korean by*
Mattho Mandersloot

*First published by*
Strangers Press, Norwich, 2019
part of UEA Publishing Project

*Distributed by*
NBN International
10 Thornbury Road
Plymouth PL6 7PP
t. +44 (0)1752 202301
e.cservs@nbninternational.com

*Printed by*
Swallowtail, Norwich

*Series editors*
Nathan Hamilton & Deborah Smith

*Editorial assistance*
Senica Maltese

*Cover design and typesetting*
Glen Robinson

Illustration and Design Copyright © Glen Robinson, 2019

ISBN: 978-1-911343-64-6

Yeoyu ——
new voices
Korea

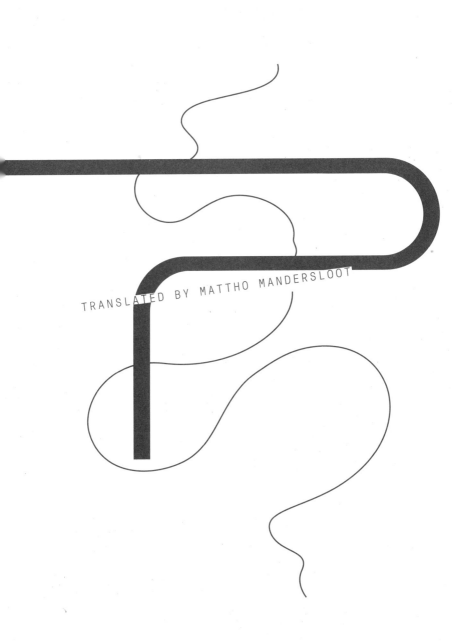

TRANSLATED BY MATTHO MANDERSLOOT

# DEMONS

***Tok.*** A sound. I looked behind me. Nothing. Misheard, maybe. I turned back and took another step to reach the front gate. *Tok*. Again, a sound like a massive rock thudding against a wall. I whipped around. This time there was something there, something small. But, in a flash, it was gone, disappeared into the alleyway. An eerie sensation burrowed into my chest. As I hurried through the gate and into the yard, Mother-in-law's sharp voice pierced my eardrums.

'*Ya!* What kept you so long?'

I approached the veranda without answering. I'd forgotten to leave work early, after she'd nagged me all morning about today's meeting, where it was to be decided when the village would gather to cook the next batch of *meju*. She got on my nerves like that. I was going to try and explain that I had work to do and couldn't come with her but ultimately couldn't be bothered. Too tired. It had been one of those days: the kids had ganged up and shoved a load of snowballs down Daejin's pants, completely soaking his underwear. I made the whole class stay behind after school and grilled them over who had started it. As I looked at each in turn, testing them one after the other, only Yongkwon had the guts to hold my gaze. He was clever, by far the most charming boy in school – a bear of a ten-year-old at that – and popular with pretty much everyone. I knew better. Whenever something went down, he was behind it. As always, he wore a look of utter innocence, which, as soon as our eyes met, twisted into a sneaky grin.

I'd yet to catch him red-handed, so I had nothing to prove his guilt, but it was clear that Yongkwon was the ringleader when it came to bullying Daejin. As a teacher, with only seven kids per class, you just know. Once I happened to witness Yongkwon full-on bulldozing Daejin to the ground, but before I could even open my mouth to tell him off, Yongkwon beat me to it: 'I'm sorry, Miss Kim. It was an accident.' And then to Daejin: 'Hey, I'm sorry, Daejin. I really didn't see you.' I didn't buy any of it. I put Yongkwon in detention. Had him do a bit of self-reflection. A few days later, the mirror in the girls' toilet was covered in graffiti: *KIM MIYOUNG = CRAZY BITCH*.

Because I hadn't bothered to make any excuses, Mother-in-law seemed to take great offence. In a disapproving tone, she stressed that Mijanae from next door had left for the meeting ages ago. Why should I care? I frowned unintentionally; she was being particularly annoying today. Mijanae, an older lady who made a living by fixing bits and bobs around the village, had built quite the reputation for diligence. Everyone knew how to find her. By force of circumstance, Mijanae's daughter had left her son in Mijanae's care and of course this little guy was Daejin. Every time I looked at Mijanae, I felt a kind of helplessness, a mixture of pity and guilt. Mother-in-law felt differently. 'That hag of a woman, surely you can see she's playing games? Making everyone feel sorry for her, just so she can take advantage,' she would say, or words to that effect.

In reality, it was all about the mayor. A few years ago, he'd been enterprising enough to commercialise the village's *meju* production. On top of our annual supply for personal use, prepared once per year, *meju* was now produced throughout the winter as well, when farmers had little else to do. Care was taken only to plan work on 'days without demons', so as to avoid the

# DEMONS

interference of so-called *son*. When Mina and I had first moved to the village, I remember asking: 'Ommo, what actually are "*son*"?'

'Evil, evil spirits. Demons who come to our village to ruin things. So it's better to make our *meju* on days they're not around.'

The mayor had been responsible for liaising with the workers and, as a trusted champion of our produce, had gained in popularity through his reorganisation of the production process. Without him at the helm, the village might not have survived. Now, a man of such excellent repute and impeccable manners, who coincidentally had wound up a widower five years ago, was precisely the kind of man to win Mother-in-law's affection. But whenever he had an errand that needed running, it was Mijanae he called on. Hence Mother-in-law's disdain.

'*Ya*, are you deaf?' she said, again sharply.

Mother-in-law was never the type to lose it at me, but she would brook no contradiction. She never *asked* me to come home early. As a rule, she would only ever *command*.

I changed the subject. 'Ommo, where's Mina?'

'Sleeping, in her room. She dropped off the minute I picked her up from nursery.'

'Pardon?'

A few days ago, we'd spoken about changing Mina's sleeping pattern. I'd asked why she thought Mina had so much trouble falling asleep at night, which I already knew was due to her habitual nap after nursery. Mother-in-law, having no taste for responsibility, retorted that *she* couldn't help it if the girl was tired in the day, that *I* shouldn't raise my child with such an iron fist and there's no need to be so harsh. She ignored the fact that, by letting Mina take a nap, she conveniently had her hands free to prepare *banchan* – dried radish leaves, sliced sweet potato, and so on – which she might later present to the mayor. So, come nightfall, I was the one having to hush and lull a wide-awake little girl, her little eyes sparkling with energy. I'd only moved to this far-flung corner of the country because I'd believed Mother-in-law's offer to help look after her. So the promise had meant nothing? My complaint seemed to get through to her, and she'd relented; no more naps.

But now here she was again putting Mina to bed during daylight hours. I was about to ask for an explanation as to why she would break a promise she had only just made when she headed me off: 'Did Yongkwon do well today? Isn't he the sweetest thing?'

As it happened, Yongkwon was the mayor's grandson. I'd had enough; yesterday, I'd received a call from my husband saying he might need to extend his secondment in Indonesia, and now this. 'Enjoy the meeting,' I said and went to my room.


The village is a dot on the horizon. Driving along the highway, flanked on both sides by green paddy fields that glimmer in the sun, you might notice the expanse of grassland briefly interrupted. As you wonder how much further the earth might stretch, the road slowly dips and narrows. After a while, a run-down shopping area appears. Still further down, you stumble upon a forest path, densely overgrown with bamboo, with leaves so thick and stems so slanted overhead, it feels as though you're in a tunnel, so much does it conceal the sky and shut out all the light.

On the other side of that you will find the village. Living here by a river at the foot of a mountain, your lungs billow with crisp, clean air. The average temperature is much lower than the city. During winters such as this, you feel every inch of your body freeze.

'Mommy look!' said Mina.

# DEMONS

I lifted my head. We'd somehow found ourselves at the apex of the bridge across the mountain river. Below us, two black goats grazed at leisure. The bridge is the first thing you see as you approach the village. On its far side is the village hall, where Mother-in-law would be. Opposite it, and its reek of economic development, stands a Japanese shrine, and it's here people gather to perform *jesa* on *meju*-making days. Elsewhere, every roof in the village is covered in identical blue *hanok* tiles, as though the village were one big complex, and one in a state of such frailty it might crumble at any moment.

'Mommy, that goat is black!' said Mina.

I stroked her hair. She had on a smile that seemed unlikely ever to fade, so long as she could dart around and look at goats. She'd only learned how to say 'goat' recently but pronounced it well. She had started talking long before most of her peers and often followed her grandmother around, striking up conversations with adults. As a result, her turns of phrase varied wildly and sometimes she would talk like me, sometimes like her grandma, then other times like Mijanae or Mijanae's neighbour, Miss Song.

On one occasion, I realised she was doing a flawless impersonation of the mayor and, even more dangerous, sometimes she would practice vocabulary I'd never taught her. Despite her charm, she could look fearsome spitting out words she must've learned from villagers, taking on a subtle hint of their accent.

*Am I raising my child the right way?* Sometimes I felt my head would split open from such worries and, with my husband so far away, I now found myself at a complete loss. And yet I felt suffocated to think of him. Whenever he'd call, we'd end up fighting. This time he'd begun by saying his company was short of staff and so it would be irresponsible for him to come back to Korea right now. But what about Mina; what about us?

He'd let out a long sigh. 'I thought you wanted me to take this job?'

But it's always been like that between us. When he decided to take the position, I held up the pretence that I was fine, but, in truth, I was worried senseless about having to raise a child with no one else around, while he stood up against the competition like he felt he had to. Around that time Mother-in-law had called and I'd welcomed her proposal. Sooner or later, I'd thought, Mina would end up living with her grandmother. I'd wanted to calm my husband's fears about leaving his ageing mother. Besides, I'd thought country life would be easy as a teacher: class sizes were small and there was less administrative rigmarole to worry about. Then after being away for a year, he goes ahead and extends his secondment without consulting me. I was at a loss for words, unable even to move my lips.

'You think I'm only doing this for me?' he said.

I told him not to get in touch for a while and hung up.

'*Ya!* Hey, goaty! Look here, you stupid!'

Mina suddenly slammed her hand against the railing, producing a loud bang. I put her down on her own feet immediately and told her sternly to stop and not say such things. She shook her head and pulled a long face while pressing her lips together, just like her father. Something had clearly got into her. Fatigue? Given her aptitude with words, I'd often make the mistake of thinking she understood things she couldn't. Sometimes she knew exactly what she was saying, but more often than not she would regurgitate words and phrases she happened to overhear. As I stood debating how might she have come across such a phrase, I heard the sound again.

# DEMONS

*Tok.* Startled, I turned to look behind me. Nothing. No one in sight but Mina and me. A chilling gust of wind dove down the nape of my neck, sprouting goosebumps over my back.

'Why can't I? The goat's a darky!' Mina said.

'What?' I looked around again. Luckily, we were still alone.

'Mina, who told you that? You can't say things like that. Don't ever say that again, you hear me?'

'Why?'

'It's a bad word.'

'Why? Isn't he a darky? He's black, isn't he?'

'Mina, I told you not to say that again.'

'Why?'

I grabbed her hand and pulled her close. We needed to go home right away. Where on earth had she picked *that* up? Was this the first time she'd said it out loud? Maybe she's been shouting it for days, maybe other people had heard her say it too. Could she have got it from Mother-in-law? No, she wasn't the type, but I was still annoyed with her. Had she looked after Mina properly, this probably wouldn't have happened. Didn't she understand how she was bound to pick up those kinds of words if she was too exposed to the rest of the village?

Here she was saying I was too strict of a parent while she used the same dishrag to clean the sink then wipe Mina's plate, printed fat layers of lipstick on her cheek whenever she felt so inclined, and, to top it off, left the girl to her own devices to the point where she'd pick up words like that... And *I'm* the crazy one? What do you mean, 'days without demons'? I can't remember the last time I had one.

I drew Mina closer. 'Time to go home now.'

Mina demanded more goats and prepared to throw herself on the ground before I lifted her up and carried her. She squirmed and kicked in my arms, until all of a sudden she became completely still. I let out a long sigh. I might now have the hang of teaching, I might even have made it my job, but raising a child of my own, it was all too clear I didn't understand the creatures in the slightest.

'Mommy, I told you I saw a darky,' Mina said to the back of my head.

In the middle of my chest, it felt as though a knot disentangled and exploded. I put Mina down again and was close to yelling at her but froze as I sensed a glower behind me. Slowly, I turned around.

From the other side of the bridge, barely five steps away, a familiar face was looking in our direction. When had he got here? I swallowed nervously as he continued to stare straight at me.

'Miss Kim,' he said.

With difficulty, I moulded my face into a smile. 'Ah, Yongkwon, on your way home, are you?'

'Yes.'

We were surrounded by perfect silence. The icy echo of his voice had left me with goosebumps again. Had he overheard? And if so, what? I nodded vaguely towards him. 'Well, off you go then,' I said and started walking away at a quickening pace with Mina resting quietly in my arms. Before turning into the nearest alleyway, I glanced back and Yongkwon was still standing there, as if keeping watch. I walked even faster. *Don't say a word. Mina, don't you dare say a word.*


That night I was woken up by a clattering noise in the yard. As with most houses here, our yard was fenced off with an iron gate, which I always secured with a chain. Even so, anyone could jump over it. I went out onto the veranda. There wasn't the faintest source of light between our house and the gate. A fluorescent tube hanging beneath the roof casted a dim shimmer, but it didn't reach as far as the yard. From where I stood, it was impossible to know what was happening on the other side.

'Who's there?' I shouted.

The gate shook vigorously. *Clang-tonk*. Someone must be trying to break in. Little by little, the noise intensified. *Thump, thump*. The chain sounded like it might burst any moment now. Should I call the police? It would take them a while to get all the way out here, but...

'*Ya, ya*, what are you doing out there?'

Mother-in-law. At once, the trembling subsided and the quiet returned.

'Ommo, didn't you hear that noise?'

'What noise?'

I stared blindly into the dark. 'I... don't know.'

Mother-in-law clicked her tongue and turned away. 'Come, let's go back in.' I shook my head and snatched a flashlight from my desk drawer. 'You stay with Mina,' I told her, grabbing my shoes. 'Where are you going?' she asked, but I didn't answer. 'Where are you going!' she repeated. Pointing my flashlight at the gate, I crept across the yard. The locks were still in place. It couldn't have been that serious. As long as the gate stayed shut, everything would be fine.

Carefully, I touched my hand to its cold, firm surface. A flesh-like, metallic odour hit my nostrils, and, *tok*, something smacked against the gate again, shaking it to and fro. I gave a shriek and staggered backwards as, *swoosh*, something stole away. Though my field of vision was narrowed, I could clearly see something. Someone's heel, I suspected, or the tail of some animal as it disappeared down the alleyway in the direction of Mijanae's house. I sighed deeply and watched my breath turn white and disperse in the cold air until there was nothing left.

I was relieved to find Mina fast asleep. Standing by the window, I watched Mother-in-law as she stroked her hair. I listened to the wind outside as I recalled what had happened earlier at the bridge. It worried me, but it wasn't necessarily something that needed her involvement right now.

'Mijanae's been acting very strange lately,' Mother-in-law started of her own accord.

'Oh,' I responded absentmindedly. She barely managed to go two days without slandering the old woman at the best of times and I was still caught up in thinking about Yongkwon and the way he had stared at me. It made me feel uneasy. I considered what he might have said when he got home. Whether he would tell his parents about Mina and me, about what she'd said. He could easily spread a rumour. 'I heard our teacher's daughter say this and that. She must have got it from her mother.' How on earth did Mina even know that word in the first place?

'Yes, she keeps saying weird things about the mayor.'

'Yeah?' As I gave another half-hearted answer, Daejin's face suddenly came to mind – that expression he had when he couldn't look me in the eye – and my head jerked up at the surprise of it.

'Hang on, say that again?'

As if she'd been waiting for the invitation, Mother-in-law launched into a full tirade. Apparently the mayor had been asking for Mijanae's help too often, but whenever she found the time to go see him, he never actually had any work for her and instead would offer her a cup of tea and try to make conversation, much to Mijanae's irritation. 'Can't he see I'm busy? If I'd been able to spend all this time working, I could have bought Daejin an extra snack.'

After a month or so of this, the situation got even worse. In response to his umpteenth request, Mijanae arrived at his house to find all of his family out. He offered her tea, as usual, but this time she said she was too busy and couldn't stay. Venturing a smile, he protested that all he wanted was her advice about finding a new manager to oversee the production of *meju*, so she felt she had no choice but to go sit with him and, as she did, he presented her with a white envelope. Her earnings, he said, and – why not? – a small bonus. Mijanae accepted the envelope with both hands and tuned out while he prattled on further. Uh-huh, uh-huh, uh-huh. She made no effort to feign interest, then all of a sudden he'd jumped up from his seat saying he'd forgotten he had a small present for her. In one long stride, he'd moved behind her back and she'd heard him open a cupboard. Dust scattered through the air and prickled her nose. She was about to sneeze when, without any warning, the mayor's hands appeared back in front of her, holding a gift-wrapped set of traditional Japanese sweets. Distracted by the cherry blossom pattern, she'd let her guard down, at which point the mayor seized the opportunity to grope her.

'Oh... my,' I was taken aback. I genuinely didn't know what else to say.

'Exactly,' Mother-in-law sighed. 'It was unbearable. I bet if she'd had the chance, she'd have gone on all day.'

'Pardon me?'

Glancing at me disapprovingly, as if to say, 'Have you not been listening at all?' Mother-in-law carried on. Mijanae had, apparently, had an ulterior motive to share this episode widely. She'd wanted everyone to think that she'd wound the mayor around her finger, the stupid hag, but she had it all wrong. Clearly she didn't realise the mayor was only being nice to her out of pity and how dare she spread such blatant gossip? I sensed a kind of thrill behind the rant.

'Ommo, did you tell this to anyone else? You didn't, did you?'

The exaggerated surprise at my question was answer enough. She might not have told anyone else just yet, but she was all too eager to do so in order that she might convince the world Mijanae had lost her mind. I suggested the story didn't exactly flatter the mayor either. It was understandable she had assumed Mijanae's version was nonsense, because she wouldn't dream of questioning the mayor, but how could she be confident everyone else might draw the same conclusion?

'Will you use your brains for once?' she snapped and jumped to her feet.

'Ommo, are you absolutely sure Mijanae said those things?'

'Do you ever listen to me? Do you think I can't tell fact from fiction? I told you exactly what she said, word for word!' She jerked the door open and left the room, howling insults as she went. Mina grumbled in her sleep. As I rubbed her chest in gentle circles, her breath returned to a peaceful rhythm. She had always been difficult to wake.

One reason I'd found the story so hard to believe was that Mijanae never so much as opened her mouth to anyone; most of her interactions consisted of stealing shy glances and, even if the person she was with clearly didn't bear her any ill will, she wouldn't drop her guard, wary as she was of any potential rumours. It's not that Mother-in-law was altogether unreliable but to think she'd sat through this whole story without feeling the slightest sympathy for Mijanae also seemed fairly unlikely and, further, if Mijanae had wanted to open up to someone, why of all people would she have picked her? None of it added up.

Again Daejin's face flashed into my mind, how he looked away whenever he got scared or whenever he was lying. On the day of the graffiti incident, he had come to see me, alone. He had said he was the one who'd written it. He'd been angry because class had finished late. I looked at him in disbelief and said 'okay'. When he turned around to walk away, I noticed he was limping. I called him back, stopping him in his tracks. Avoiding my gaze, he'd explained: 'I fell down the stairs. It was an accident'. I couldn't do anything to help him because he'd lied to me and refused to take me into his confidence. He wouldn't tell me what happened to him, who beat him up, who gave the orders to shove snowballs down his pants. No matter how hard I tried getting such information out of him, it was no use. Why didn't he trust me?

Though he might trust his grandmother. Perhaps he talked to her. It would explain many things: if Mijanae had found out what Daejin went through at school, it might explain why she went around telling stories about the mayor. Indeed the scandal may have been her fabrication, but I wasn't quite convinced. Mother-in-law took it as a given; she blamed Mijanae for merely existing and given the slightest chance to demean her, she'd grab at it with both hands. Whichever way you looked at it, if word got out, the mayor was in big trouble.

*Pssh, how silly to let my thoughts wander so.* What was certain was this: Daejin was being bullied and I could do nothing about it. Whether his grandmother had a habit of muttering abuse when she was alone was a matter of speculation. When people get cross, they say stuff they normally wouldn't. Stuff about the mayor, in Mijanae's case, or even stuff about Yongkwon. Before she knows, she's said 'darky' this and 'darky' that. It wouldn't stop her if there was a three-year-old in her vicinity who might quote her every word. Who knows, she might even have *wanted* Mina to hear. 'Go on then, say what I just said. Say it whenever you want.'

Darkness filled the room. My thoughts kept whirling as I watched Mina sleep. Mother-in-law had combed her hair to one side and I noticed her slightly protruding forehead as if for the first time. It was a feature we shared. I sighed and lay down beside her but still couldn't put my mind at ease. Perhaps it was worth having a word with Mijanae.


All the different shades of stink that the village had to offer crowded Mijanae's house: the musty tang of dried pepper, the foul stench of *meju*, the rotten odour of parched radish leaves. Mijanae was kind enough to let me in, even though I arrived unannounced, and on a Sunday morning at that. She sat in front of me with trembling lips, apprehensive as to the purpose behind my visit.

I handed her the box of confectionery I'd brought. 'I owe you an apology,' I began. 'My mother-in-law and daughter come to your house so often and I've never even introduced myself.'

'I should be the one apologising,' she said shyly, waving her hand. 'I'm sorry to leave Daejin so much in your care.' She had a mild, pliable air to her, as I'd expected she would.

I asked if Daejin was around. Gone out to play with friends, she answered. I'd always assumed Daejin had no friends to play with after school, to protect him. But knowing that most kids went to *hakwon* after class and the rest went straight home, I'd set my mind at rest. Daejin had nothing to worry about. Whatever might happen outside of school, he wasn't in real danger, though hearing that Daejin was out with 'friends' still made me feel a little uncomfortable.

# DEMONS

'Miss Kim, are you sure you're doing okay?'

I smiled awkwardly. I hadn't expected this question and didn't understand what she was aiming at. With a solemn face, she added: 'Kids these days, they're such troublemakers...'

I understood: this was about the graffiti incident. Ever since it happened, I'd kept getting vaguely compassionate remarks whenever people ran into me: 'So many kids have problems nowadays. But in our village, they're so sweet. Don't you think?'

The words still haunted me. They'd been written in huge characters across the whole length of the mirror. In the middle of class, I'd grabbed a cloth from the office and wiped the mirror clean with my own hands. I said nothing about it, not a word. I suspected Mijanae didn't know that Daejin had later confessed. Otherwise she would presumably have come to speak to me herself. Or maybe she'd wanted to all along but couldn't. Either way, she now looked utterly perturbed. A part of me felt heartbroken.

I smiled. I was fine, thank you.

'I'm glad. Yongkwon is such a keen student, you see,' she said tenderly.

At the beginning of the year, I had given the kids a short spelling quiz, after which we were to go over their mistakes. In general, they all found the same things difficult, so inevitably my discussion focused on mistakes they all had made. I was summoned by the head-teacher the next day. Yongkwon's parents had called. It had been reported that I had picked on Yongkwon. I had held up a stack of Yongkwon's answer papers and read each and every one of his mistakes aloud. 'That's wrong, and that, and that, and that. You aren't as clever as people think, are you now, Yongkwon?' and so on. Then, waving one of his papers in the air, I had said: 'Yongkwon, you are absolutely terrible at writing. You really have to brush up on your grammar if you want to stay with us.'

Not true.

Simply not true.

'He's just doing his best,' Mijanae said.

I wasn't sure whether it actually happened or I imagined it because of how her words made me feel, but I watched Mijanae's expression turn to stone as she finished her sentence. I felt glued to my seat and clasped my hands. Why would Mijanae bring this up now? I didn't understand.

'Everyone knows what you said about Yongkwon,' said Mijanae. 'But he's the sweetest thing. He really is, isn't he?'

I wasn't having this. 'Daejin might disagree with you on that, actually.'

My reason for coming had been to offer my help and to ask about what hardships might she be going through; to tell her about Daejin's problems at school and to build a sense of mutual trust in order to find a joint solution. I'd also wanted to ask about Mina and pick up on anything that might explain how she had come to use swear words, so I might prevent its ever happening again. That's what I'd come here to do. It's what I had to do.

That's the truth.

The honest truth.

I suppressed something of a storm of emotion in order to continue with equanimity. I cushioned the painful details for her own sake, voicing my 'suspicion' that Daejin didn't really get along with the other kids at school. That he wouldn't speak up, not even if he was in trouble. Cautiously, I mentioned how Yongkwon bullied him. As I did so, Mijanae looked me up and down from out of the corner of her eye. 'And it is when those two boys are together that Daejin seems to struggle the most,' I continued.

Mijanae cut me off. 'Miss Kim, have you *seen* any of this with your own eyes?'

# DEMONS

For a moment, I was a little dumbfounded and I hesitated. But she left me no choice but to tell her the whole story. Bracing myself, I proceeded to tell her about the day Daejin came to see me. How he had told me *he* was behind the graffiti, but I hadn't believed him and how I had got the feeling something else was the matter. I was about to add that he had looked absolutely terrified, when Mijanae, in a strange tone, said: 'But Miss Kim, Daejin was off school at the time because of his leg, remember?'

'Daejin came to see me after school, I'm positive. Feel free to ask him yourself,' I shot back.

Mijanae was sceptical. But how could she be? This conversation was about a part of her grandson's life she wasn't privy to. As her only source, I hadn't anticipated Mijanae would simply refuse to take me at my word. I recalled Mother-in-law's story regarding how the mayor was always asking after Mijanae and how she'd bragged about it. 'If she'd had the chance, she'd have gone on all day.' I decided to change tack.

'If I may be so bold, how do you get on with the mayor?'

That moment, the gate slid open. *Creeek*. And, *tok*, the thudding was back. As one, Mijanae and I turned our heads. The front door was closed, but through the window I could see a shadow – a silhouette – flicker outside. Something was moving around the veranda. Perhaps Daejin had come home. But no, he would presumably yell 'hello' to his grandma or some such thing and come straight in as opposed to skulking. Looking through the window, I followed the swift movements of the dark form, small and short. When I turned back to Mijanae to ask if she'd seen it too, I noticed her eyes were sunken. She was pressing her wrinkled lips together, her gaze intent on the door. Her fists rested on her knees, as though she were trying to squeeze something to pulp, and one of the veins of her hand was popping. I had seen the expression before, on the day Daejin had come to see me. He had had precisely the same look on his face as he avoided my eyes: the anxious look of someone with something to hide.

I reached out and grabbed her fist. She flinched.

'Is everything okay?' I asked.

She yanked her arm away, shaking off my grip, and looked down at the floor. I sensed the thing outside slowly retreating. *Tomorrow must be a day without demons, then. A bright, clear day without any trouble.*

Mijanae's voice crawled out of her mouth as she continued to stare at the floor: 'I'm sorry, but you're acting very strangely, Miss Kim. You keep pretending something's the matter.'

Outside, all was silence.


The villagers had gathered at dawn in front of the Japanese shrine. The *meju*-making had been scheduled to begin after the *jesa*. Women were not supposed to perform ceremonial bows, but Mina happened to be standing with a group of men and automatically followed their lead, bringing her little forehead all the way down to touch the floor. After rising up again, she tiptoed to the offering table to steal a boiled egg. Everyone laughed. Children are innocent. They can get away with anything.

Mina looked happy. As she roamed through the crowd, she bumped someone's leg and they smiled and said something apparently nice to her, indulging her antics before she bumbled on to play with the next. I was ill at ease. I couldn't shake the fear she might blurt another swear word. If it were up to me, I'd have taken her home right then. Unfortunately, that would have upset Mother-in-law and it was unlikely Mina would co-operate in any case. I decided to hang around for the time being, but stood to one side like a piece of furniture, making sure my desire to leave was obvious enough. I had offered to lend a hand, but my help had been waved away. It wasn't necessary, they said. They made it sound as if they were being considerate, but really they just didn't want my alien claws ruining their work. But if I were to leave so soon, I'd only be criticised for that too, so I stayed put, waiting for the height of the commotion to find Mina and be gone.

'Everyone into the village hall!' An endless row of wheelbarrows filled with water-soaked beans passed by in single file as the announcement rang out. Moist air rising up from the pots would circulate to every corner and the smell of boiling beans would permeate the village, leaving a delicate trace of warmth. Today was the only day in the year when our glacial village would thaw.

I took Mina into the hall. It had been reorganised when the mayor set up his business and a few enormous stoves were installed where originally a small one outside had sufficed. When it comes to making *meju*, there is no point boiling beans for just an hour or two. You have to stoop over your pot for an entire day stirring continuously, so the mush doesn't stick to the bottom. Then it must be mashed until it turns yellow. It is part of the village's method to then put the mash in a clean rubber basin, pound it stiff, mould it into individual bricks, and leave them to dry on a bed of rice straw. All this was to be done today.

As work got underway and everyone started busying themselves, I thought it might be our chance to leave, but Mina had other ideas as she drove her way deeper into the crowd.

'Mina-ya!'

I called her back at the top of my voice. It was pointless. I may as well have been shouting to myself. I felt a cold sweat break across my back. I now wanted nothing more than to take her home. I hastened my step.

From the corner of my eye I caught sight of Mother-in-law and Mijanae, busily engaged. Mijanae stood in front of a stove, stirring a pot of beans; Mother-in-law was having an animated conversation with the mayor, smiling up at him as she was wont to do. I couldn't believe what I saw next. Taking a step to the side, the mayor briefly rested his hand on Mijanae's waist. She flinched and looked around her. Was she laughing? No, frowning? I couldn't read her face. Then Mother-in-law pulled a long-handled scoop from out of the pot of beans, used it to strike Mijanae on the top of her foot, and strode briskly out of the hall.

The strike caused Mijanae to drop to the floor and curl up into a ball, but if she was in any pain she managed not to cry out. I wondered whether I should go check on her or whether it was better to run after Mother-in-law. I wavered a while, then was forced to abandon either option as Mina moved back into sight no more than ten steps away from me, with another kid by her side.

The child stood very close to her, lowered his head, whispered something in her ear. Was that... Yongkwon?

I took off at such a sprint my feet barely touched the ground. I crashed into someone's shoulder not even halfway there and for a second the only thing I could see was the ceiling. When I turned my head back to look ahead, Mina was gone. Wonderful timing.

'Mina-ya!' I shouted.

Everyone turned to look at me. I checked around, but she wasn't to be seen. No Yongkwon, either. I called her name again, then I called his, my voice cracking with fright. *I saw them here just now, they were right here a second ago.* But the throng of people wouldn't listen. Instead, a man walked up to me and requested that I be quiet. He wouldn't get out of my way until I shouted at him.

# DEMONS

Everyone looked at me like I was mad. Not a soul would help me find Mina. I scanned the area for Mother-in-law now, but there was no sign of her either. Fighting through the hubbub, I kept yelling Mina's name, until someone tapped me on the shoulder.

'Miss Kim?'

I jerked around so quickly that the woman shrunk back. She was small and dark-skinned. It was Yongkwon's mother.

I took a long breath and sighed, looking deeply into her eyes. In some inexplicable way, they seemed to communicate something to me. They carried something within them.

'Where's Yongkwon?'

She simply shook her head. I wanted to grab her hair and shake her to bits. *Tell me where your son is, right now. Tell me you know what the hell he's doing to my daughter. Say something, at the very least. You've never said a single word to me, for all the time I've lived here.* I was beside myself and ready to bombard her with threats. To use my fists if necessary. After all, she deserved it. But as I took a step in her direction, I heard a sound, now familiar, coming from outside the building. *Tok. Tok.*

I ran outside and a few people followed. The sound seemed to be coming from the small stove on the opposite side of the building. I turned the corner, but the closer I got the more aware I became of a strange smell, somewhere between foul and damp. Smoke fumes rose in the distance and scattered on the ground were pieces of worn clothing, paper scraps, half-scorched rice straws, lumps of bean mash, piles of dirt. The smell lingered in my nose.

The back wall was covered with stripes of coal. I heard a giggle. Yongkwon and Daejin were sitting in front of the small stove.

*Tok.*

It came from bundles of dry bamboo, stuck into the fire pit. Air bubbles frothed from inside the branches as they popped like firecrackers. As soon as the two of them saw me, they started to their feet.

'Where's Mina?' I asked Yongkwon, calmly.

Pretending not to know what I meant, he looked at me unmoved, with that familiar, stoic smile on his face. I curbed my mounting anger and asked, again calmly: 'What's all this on the ground?'

After exchanging eye contact with Daejin, Yongkwon answered: 'We were just playing. It got a bit messy.' He paused. 'I'm sorry. It was an accident.'

I charged at Yongkwon, grabbing him by the shoulders and shaking him. 'What did you do to Mina, where did you take her?' Yongkwon burst into tears. 'I don't know, Miss, I don't know.' His voice brimmed with fear. I could no longer bear to look at this mask of his. I wanted to see his real face. I had to. I couldn't stop myself, but someone else did, grabbing my arms from behind.

It was Yongkwon's mother. She pushed me over and I lost my balance, letting go of her son in the process. She rushed to embrace him, all the while managing to glare at me. Daejin was still standing next to him.

'Mina's grandma took her home,' he stammered. 'We just told you! We saw her walk off with her grandma and the mayor.'

He wouldn't look me in the eye. His gaze was fixed instead at some point in mid-air. I knew it. It wasn't true. It was simply not true. I staggered back to my feet and still he looked away. I wanted to reach out to him, but someone's voice interrupted.

'Excuse me, but I saw Mina go home too.'

I looked behind me. The whole village was staring at me with the exact same expression on their faces, like how the tiles on their houses were all dyed the exact same shade of blue. For a moment, no one said anything.

# DEMONS

Someone broke the silence. 'Go see for yourself.' Others chimed in. 'Always known she was cuckoo.' 'How can she get so upset over nothing?' Rooted to the spot, I could do nothing but listen in silence. 'Thanks for ruining the day.' Drained of all energy, I muttered: 'I'm sorry.'

I bowed my head to Yongkwon's mother. 'I think I've misjudged the situation. I'm very sorry.'

I felt another pang of self-loathing, as she refused to reply.

Yet, I couldn't get rid of the feeling that something wasn't right. I couldn't understand why Mother-in-law would have taken Mina home, and without telling me. But what else could I do at this point?

Another voice spoke behind my back: 'Looking for Mina?'

Nodding my head, I turned around.

'Isn't that a coincidence,' said the voice. 'I think I saw her walk off with Mijanae. She seemed to be crying.'

I turned my head quickly and my gaze crossed Daejin's. He didn't avoid it this time.

'Who said that? Who was that just now?' I asked, with a quivering voice.

No one answered. I then recalled Mother-in-law's face and her malicious smile as she struck Mijanae's foot. Yes, and I recalled Mijanae's face too, her teeth clenched in pain. I was suddenly sure of that now.

I made off again, this time in the direction of Mijanae's.


Our house stood on a low hill at a reasonable distance from the village hall and Mijanae's was just below. All the houses on the hill were pretty much identical, one standing next to the other, but I never realised they were so far away. My chest heaved, my heart pounded. I felt something tug my ankle and fell to the ground, then a heavy burden of fear also crushing on my back. I drew a breath, got back to my feet, and headed up the hill.

The front gate to Mijanae's house was open. 'Mina-ya!' I shouted, as I approached the front door.

No answer. I opened the door and stepped inside, tumbling again to the floor before I could even plant my foot. I felt something squash under the weight of my palms and jumped back to my feet. It was a lump of bean mash. Multiple lumps of bean mash. The moisture squeezed from the lump with my fall was now all over my pants. Calling out to Mina again, I looked around the room but couldn't find the light switch. There was nothing in this pitch-black room but the smell of squashed beans. I lifted my head and noticed a few spotty areas on the wall. It seemed as though mould had gathered all around the room. The whole house was like a brick of rotten *meju*, covered in white mould. Last time I was here, talking with Mijanae, the rotten smell was confined to one corner of the room. I could see something in that corner now. It was completely dark, but I was able to see it clearly.

The day of the graffiti incident, after I'd cleaned up the mirror and returned to the classroom, I didn't talk about it in front of the class. I made them stay after hours every day. I didn't tell them why, I didn't tell them for how long, I just made them sit at their desks in silence, doing nothing. They formed a pact, firm as a *meju* brick, boiled to the taste of this village. They felt no need to break the silence because they spoke with their eyes. *Let's get this over with, let's do whatever it takes to end this.* I was well aware that they took their conversations outside the classroom. I knew they were deciding which one of them would take the blame, selecting their sacrifice, their peace offering to allay my anger. I could tell they were up to something, there was plenty of time for them to conspire. And I knew it would take more than words to settle the matter. Such was the harsh reality. As a teacher, with only seven kids per class, you just know. One of the following days, I kept them at school until late in the evening and received a call from one of their parents. 'So many kids have problems nowadays,' I laughed into the horn. 'But in our village, they're so sweet. Don't you think?'

I heard something. Was it Mina? I looked around, calling out her name. But my voice was absorbed by the silence. As I turned my head, whatever I'd seen in the corner had vanished. Again, a waft of that rotten smell. I had to figure out where it came from and why it was following me around. Did it issue from this particular room? This particular house? Was the whole damned village infused with it? After all, why would demons want to meddle with people's lives in the first place? It was anyone's guess. I slowly buried my face in the hollow of my hands and inhaled, sucking the rotten smell deep into my lungs. I knew what it was. It all made sense now.

**Yeoyu** is a series of chapbooks showcasing the work of some of the most exciting writers working in Korean today, published by Strangers Press, part of the UEA Publishing Project.

여유

**Yeoyu** is a unique collaboration between an international group of independent creative practitioners, with University of East Anglia, Norwich University of the Arts, and the National Centre for Writing, made possible by LTI Korea.

University of East Anglia

NORWICH
UNIVERSITY
OF THE ARTS